Ravenscourt
B·O·O·K·S

Jack London's

The Call of the Wild

Retold by

Barbara Wood

Illustrated by

Gary Torrisi

Columbus, OH • Chicago, IL • Redmond, WA

The McGraw·Hill Companies

SRAonline.com

 SRA

Copyright © 2004 by SRA/McGraw-Hill.

All rights reserved. Except as permitted under the United States Copyright Act, no part of this publication may be reproduced or distributed in any form or by any means, or stored in a database or retrieval system, without the prior written permission of the publisher, unless otherwise indicated.

Send all inquiries to:
SRA/McGraw-Hill
8787 Orion Place
Columbus, OH 43240-4027

Printed in the United States of America.

ISBN 0-07-601602-1

3 4 5 6 7 8 9 MAL 08 07 06 05 04

Chapter 1

Trouble

Buck did not read the newspapers, or he would have known that trouble was coming. There would be trouble for Buck and for every dog like him. A shiny, yellow metal had been found in the Arctic. Now thousands of men were rushing to the Northland to hunt for the treasure. These men needed dogs—dogs with muscles strong enough to pull sleds, dogs with coats thick enough to stay warm in the frozen Arctic.

Buck lived at Judge Miller's place in California. Buck liked to stroll along the wide porch that wrapped around the big house. In back there were orchards, pastures, a swimming pool, and berry patches.

Buck ruled it all. He had been born here. He had lived here all four years of his life. There were other dogs, but they did not count. They came and went, living in the kennels or in the house.

But Buck was neither a house dog nor a kennel dog. The whole place was his. He went with the judge's daughters on long walks. He swam in the pool with the judge's sons. He carried the judge's grandsons on his back. And on winter nights he lay at the judge's feet by the warm fire. Buck was king. He ruled over all living things.

Buck's father, a huge Saint Bernard, had been the judge's friend. Buck was smaller like his mother, a Scottish shepherd dog. Still, he carried his one hundred and forty pounds in royal fashion. Buck was like a country gentleman, taking pride in himself. His muscles were hardened by hunting, water races, and other outdoor delights.

*In the fall of 1897, gold fever was spreading. But Buck did not read the newspapers. He did not know that Manuel, the gardener's helper, needed more money than he could earn as a gardener.

The judge was at a meeting the night Manuel stole Buck. No one saw Manuel and Buck go off through the orchard. And only one man saw them arrive at the train station. There Manuel tied a rope around Buck's neck and sold him to a stranger.

"Twist the rope and you'll choke him plenty," said Manuel.

When the stranger took Buck's rope, the dog growled. The rope tightened around his neck, cutting off his breath. In a rage Buck sprang at the man. The rope tightened as Buck struggled. He panted. Never had he been treated like this! Never had he been so angry! Yet there was nothing he could do. He was put* into a crate and thrown into the train's baggage car.

4

In the morning evil-looking men picked up the crate. Buck raged at them through the bars. The men only laughed and poked sticks at him. Buck bared his teeth and charged at them. The men laughed again. He realized this was what the men wanted, so he lay down. The crate passed through many hands. It was finally loaded into a car at the end of the train.

For two more days and nights Buck rode in the crate. He neither ate nor drank. His eyes turned bloodshot. Anger welled in his veins.

When the train stopped in Seattle, four men carried the crate into a backyard. A man in a red sweater signed some papers, and then he opened the crate. The other men scrambled to safety at the top of a wall. There they could watch the man in the red sweater.

The man in the red sweater picked up a club. Buck ground his teeth and charged at the man. Buck was about to rip into the man when a streak of pain ran through his body. Buck had never been struck with a club in his life, and he did not understand.

With a fierce snarl Buck sprang at the man again. Again a shock of pain brought him crashing to the ground. This time Buck realized that it was the club, but he didn't care. Buck charged a dozen times, and each time the club smashed him down. Finally the dog lay where he had fallen. He was too dazed and bloody to try again.

"Well, Buck, my boy," said the man in the red sweater, "you have learned your place. Be a good dog, and all will go well. Be a bad dog, and I'll whale the stuffing out of you. Understand?"

When the man patted Buck's head, Buck endured the touch without a fight. When the man brought water, Buck drank. Later Buck ate a big meal of raw meat, chunk by chunk, from the man's hand. Buck had learned a lesson he would not forget—he stood no chance against a man with a club.

As the days went by, Buck watched other dogs fight the man in the red sweater.

Sometimes after a dog had been beaten, it wagged its tail and licked the man's hand. Buck had more pride than that. Still, he knew that a man with a club must be obeyed.

Now and again strangers came. They paid money to the man in the red sweater before taking the other dogs away. One day a man looked at Buck and said, "That's some dog! How much do you want for him?"

"Three hundred, and a bargain at that, Perrault," was the prompt reply. Perrault grinned. He knew it was not an unfair sum for so fine an animal. Perrault was a mail carrier, so he wanted to find the best dogs. He knew Buck was a high-quality animal, one in a thousand. "Or, one in ten thousand," he thought to himself.

Buck saw Perrault hand money to the man in the red sweater. Buck was not surprised when Perrault led him and another dog, named Curly, away.

From a ship called the *Narwhal,* Buck and Curly watched the shoreline disappear. It was the last time Buck saw the man in the red sweater. It was the last time he saw the warm Southland. Perrault took both dogs below deck and turned them over to a man named François. Like Perrault, François was a French Canadian. They were fair men, wise in the way of dogs. Buck soon grew to respect them.

On the *Narwhal*, Buck and Curly joined two other dogs. One was a big, snow-white fellow named Spitz. Spitz had a sneaky way of smiling as he thought of a trick—for instance, when he stole Buck's food. As Buck sprang to punish him, François's whip lashed through the air, reaching the thief first. But none of Buck's food was left, other than the bone. Even so, that was fair of François, Buck decided.

The other dog, named Dave, made no advances nor did he receive any. He did not try to steal food from Buck or Curly. He was a gloomy fellow who wanted to be left alone. He ate and slept and took interest in nothing. He did not notice that the *Narwhal* rolled and pitched on the sea. When Buck and Curly grew excited, Dave just yawned and went back to sleep.

Day and night the ship's propeller throbbed in the icy waters. Each day was like every other, but the weather was growing colder. At last the propeller was quiet. Buck knew a change was at hand. François leashed the dogs and took them up on deck.

Buck's feet sank into something white and mushy. It was very much like mud but cold. He sprang back with a snort. More of this white stuff was falling through the air. He shook himself, but more of it fell upon him. He sniffed it and then licked some of it. It bit like fire, and the next instant it was gone. This puzzled Buck. He tried again, with the same results. The onlookers laughed. Buck felt ashamed because he did not understand. It was his first snow.

— Chapter 2—

A New Life

Buck's first day on the Dyea beach was like a nightmare. On the beach there was no peace, no rest, and not a moment of safety. There was a need to be always on alert. The dogs and men on the beach were different and rough. And they followed no laws but the law of the club and fang.

The dogs fought like savages. Buck had never seen dogs fight like this. His first experience taught him a lesson. Curly was the victim. In her friendly way she made advances toward a husky. The husky sprang without warning. A flash, a clip of teeth, and Curly's face was ripped open from eye to jaw. This was the wolflike manner of fighting—attack and leap away. But there was more to it than this. Thirty or forty huskies closed in on Curly, licking their chops. This is what the huskies waited for.

They surrounded her, snarling and yelping. Curly was soon buried beneath the mass of bodies. François and other men with clubs quickly scattered the dogs, but it was too late. Curly was lifeless in the bloody, trampled snow.

So that was the way. Once you went down, that was the end of you. Buck would never let this happen to him. He could see that Spitz thought this was funny. From that moment on, Buck hated him.

Before Buck recovered from this shock, he received another. François fastened him with straps and buckles. It was a harness. It was used to force Buck and the other dogs to haul firewood. Buck's dignity was hurt, but he was too wise to rebel. François was stern with his whip, and Spitz was the leader of the pack. Spitz growled and threw his weight to jerk Buck around. Buck learned easily.

*"Dat Buck," François told Perrault, "I teach him quick as anything."

Perrault, who was in a hurry to get onto the trail, soon gathered more dogs. Two of the huskies were named Billee and Joe. They were brothers, but Billee was good-natured while Joe was the opposite. Buck welcomed them. Dave ignored them. Spitz was hostile. A one-eyed dog named Sol-leks was a long, lean husky with a look that commanded such respect that even Spitz left him alone. And being left alone was all that Sol-leks wanted.

That night Buck had a great problem sleeping. He was too cold, so he decided to go to the humans' tent. When he tried to enter the tent, Perrault and François yelled. They threw cooking spoons at him. As Buck fled, a freezing wind nipped at him. He lay on the snow and tried to sleep, but the bitter cold* sent him shivering to his feet.

His teammates had disappeared. Where had they gone? Shivering, Buck circled the tent. Suddenly the snow gave way beneath his feet. There, curled under the snow in a snug ball, lay Billee. So that was the way they did it.

Buck chose a spot and dug a hole for himself. The heat from his body quickly filled the small nest, and he fell asleep.

By morning new-fallen snow had buried him. The walls of snow were pressing in from all sides. A fear of being trapped woke him. With a snarl, he jumped straight up. The snow was flying in a cloud around him.

— Chapter 3—

Taking the Lead

"What did I say?" François called to Perrault. "Dat Buck for sure learns quick as anything!" Perrault nodded.

More huskies joined the team. Soon nine dogs were in harnesses, heading up the trail toward the Dyea Canyon. Buck was glad to be moving. He was surprised at how eager the rest of the dogs were, but he was more surprised at the change in Dave and Sol-leks. They were different beasts, no longer uninterested. The entire team was alert and agreed that the work would go well.

The lead position was taken by Spitz. Buck had been placed between Dave and Sol-leks so he could learn from them. It was a hard day's run, but Buck was a good student, soon mastering the trail.

*At night an exhausted Buck made his nest in the snow and slept until the team started out early the next day. Day after day they were off at the first gray of dawn and did not pitch camp again till after dark.

Buck was always hungry, and his share of fish never seemed enough. He had been a slow eater. Now his teammates finished before he did and robbed him of his share. So Buck learned to eat as fast as the others.

And he was not above taking what did not belong to him. Once he saw a teammate steal a slice of bacon when Perrault's back was turned. The next day Buck did the same, getting away with the whole chunk. A great uproar was raised, but no one suspected him. Respect for private property was normal in the Southland, but this was a new way of* life. Buck had to adapt. He did not steal for the joy of it but because he was hungry.

Buck's muscles soon grew hard as iron. He learned to bite out the ice in his paws. His hearing became so sharp that the slightest noise woke him.

He learned by experience, and the instincts of his ancestors awakened in him. He fought with the quick snap of a wolf. And on cold nights he pointed his nose at the sky and howled at the moon.

Buck adjusted to his new life but never felt at ease. He did not pick fights. In fact he avoided them whenever possible. Spitz, however, went out of his way to bully Buck. Spitz wished to fight to the death. Early in the trip Spitz almost got his wish.

A heavy snow had forced the group to camp on the shore of a lake. A wall of rock rose at their backs. Close under the sheltering rock Buck made his nest in the snow. The campfire thawed the ice, which put the campfire out and left the group to eat supper in the dark.

Buck hated leaving his snug nest when François passed out the fish. And when Buck had finished his share and returned to his nest, he found it occupied by Spitz. Till now, Buck had avoided trouble, but this was too much. He sprang upon Spitz, and the two tangled.

"Give it to him, Buck! The dirty thief!" yelled François.

Spitz paced back and forth, waiting for a chance to spring, and Buck was just as eager. But then the unexpected happened. The camp was invaded by starving huskies that had picked up the scent of their camp from far away. As the invaders scrambled for bread and bacon, Perrault and François attacked them with clubs.

In the meantime more of the invaders had ambushed the team of dogs, pushing them back against the rock wall. Buck's head and shoulders were slashed. Dave and Sol-leks dripped with blood. At last Billee ran onto the ice with most of the team at his heels. Spitz took the chance, and he rushed at Buck. But Buck braced to keep from falling. He escaped to join the team as they fled across the lake.

At daybreak the team limped back to camp to find the invaders gone and the two men in bad tempers. Half the food supply had been stolen. The hardest part of the trail lay ahead.

It was fifty degrees below zero, but the wild water of the Thirty Mile River had not frozen solid. Perrault fell through the ice a dozen times. Each time he built a fire to dry his clothes. Once the sled broke through the ice, carrying Buck and Dave down with it. The dogs had nearly drowned.

It took six days to cover thirty terrible miles. By the time they made it to good ice, Buck was limping in pain. His feet were not yet as hard as a husky's. François made four dog-sized slippers to protect Buck's paws. Once François forgot the slippers, so Buck lay with his feet in the air and refused to move without them.

Buck never knew what would happen in camp. One morning Buck's teammate Dolly suddenly went mad. Frothing at the mouth, she sprang at Buck. Buck had never seen a dog go mad, yet he sensed trouble and fled in panic. Dolly raced after him. As the dogs raced, François's axe crashed down upon Dolly's head. Buck was panting, exhausted. Spitz, seeing another chance, sprang upon Buck, ripping his flesh to the bone. François's whip fell, and Buck watched Spitz receive the worst whipping any of the team had ever seen.

"Someday Spitz will kill dat Buck," Perrault remarked.

"Listen," answered François, "all the time I watch dat Buck. Some fine day he'll get mad and chew dat Spitz all up and spit him out on the snow. I know."

From then on it was war. Spitz knew Buck wanted the lead position on the team. Buck wanted it because of pride and because it was his nature. He got in the way whenever Spitz tried to keep the team in line. Once Spitz leaped at a dog that had failed to show up to be harnessed. Buck sprang between them, and François had to end the fight with his whip.

Soon control broke down. Spitz was no longer the great leader to be feared. Trouble was always around the corner, and at the source of that trouble was Buck. François was furious. But Buck was too clever to be caught.

One night Buck led the pack in a chase after a snowshoe rabbit. He bounded ahead in the white moonlight. The other dogs followed, except for Spitz, who left the pack and cut across a bend in the path. He leaped from a bank into the path of the rabbit and made the kill.

Buck attacked. The two dogs rolled and fought in the snow. Spitz slashed Buck across the shoulder and snarled as he backed away. In a flash Buck knew the time had come. It would be a fight to the death. Buck tried to sink his jaws into Spitz's throat. Spitz tore at him and got away. Then Spitz rushed at Buck.

A circle of dogs waited, ready to finish off whichever of the two went down. Buck rushed at Spitz again, but this time he darted low across the snow. His teeth clenched Spitz's left foreleg. There was a crunch of bone, and Spitz's left foreleg was broken. Then Buck broke Spitz's right leg.

Even with his pain and helplessness, Spitz struggled madly to keep up. But there was no hope for him. In a final rush, Buck knocked Spitz to the ground. As Buck looked on, the circle of dogs moved in for the kill.

"What did I say?" were François's words the next morning when he found Spitz missing and Buck covered with wounds. "And now we make good time. No more Spitz, no more trouble."

While Perrault packed and loaded the sled, François harnessed the dogs. When Buck trotted up to the place Spitz would have occupied as leader, François did not notice. He brought Sol-leks to the position instead. But Buck drove Sol-leks away and stood in his place.

"Eh?" François said, slapping his leg and laughing. "Look at dat Buck. He thinks he will take the job!"

François took Buck by the scruff of the neck. He dragged Buck to one side and put Sol-leks back into the lead position. But when François turned his back, there was Buck, waiting to be harnessed in the lead again.

François was angry. "I fix you!" he cried, coming back with a heavy club in his hand.

Buck retreated, but he circled the group at a distance, snarling with rage. When François called Buck to his usual place, Buck retreated from François two or three steps. François followed, and Buck retreated a few steps again. He wanted the lead position. He had earned it, and he would not be content with less.

Perrault and François ran after Buck for the better part of an hour, yelling and throwing clubs. Buck would not back down. Finally François shrugged his shoulders in a sign that they were beaten.

Sol-leks returned to his old spot, leaving a place for Buck at the front. Buck trotted proudly into position as the leader of the team. The team followed as he dashed onto the trail.

Buck took leadership. The team understood this at once. "Never such a dog as dat Buck!" François said. "Worth one thousand dollars, eh? Wouldn't you say, Perrault?" Perrault nodded.

In record time the team raced to its goal, Skaguay. Orders came, and the team was turned over to a Scotch-Indian. Like other men, François and Perrault left Buck's life for good.

The Scotch-Indian took charge, and the team headed back to Dawson. They were carrying mail to the men who had left their homes to search for gold. The team should have had a week's rest in Dawson, but in two days they returned to Skaguay.

The dogs were tired and in poor shape. The drivers grumbled because it snowed every day. This meant a soft trail and heavier pulling.

But it was Dave who suffered most of all. Something was wrong with him, but the drivers did not know what it was. They could not locate any broken bones or deep cuts. Before long, Dave was so weak that he was falling and crying out in pain.

The Scotch-Indian took Dave away from the team. He wanted to give Dave a rest by letting him run on the beaten trail behind the sled, but Dave only whimpered over the loss of his position. He had trouble keeping up with the sled. Finally Dave lay down. He was too weak to travel.

The team continued on beyond a row of trees. Here the sled halted while the Scotch-Indian slowly retraced his steps to where Dave lay. A shot rang out. The man came back, and the team started again. But Buck knew, and every dog knew, what had taken place behind the row of trees. Dave was gone.

Chapter 4

Exhaustion

Thirty days later the team arrived in Skaguay. The dogs were in wretched shape. Buck had lost weight. Sol-leks was lame and suffering. All the dogs were dead tired.

There were orders that the exhausted dogs were to be sold and fresh ones were to take their places. On the fourth morning two men from the States bought the entire team. The men, Hal and Charles, were traveling with Charles's wife, Mercedes. She was also Hal's sister.

Buck watched as his new owners loaded the sled. They tried hard, but they had no method. They rolled the tent into a huge bundle three times as large as it should have been. They packed the unwashed tin dishes.

The load was huge when Charles and Hal piled on the last few odds and ends. Others looked on and tried to offer help. "I wouldn't tote that tent along if I were you," said one man.

"It seems a mite top-heavy," said another. "Think it'll ride?"

"Certainly," Hal answered coldly, swinging his whip at the dogs. "Mush on there!" The dogs strained, but they were unable to move the sled.

"Those dogs are weak as water," said one of the onlookers. "They need a rest."

But again the whip fell on the dogs. They threw themselves forward, dug their feet into the snow, and used all their strength. After two tries, they stood still, panting. Still the sled would not move.

*Another of the onlookers spoke up. "I don't care a whoop what becomes of you, but for the dogs' sakes I just want to tell you that you can help them a mighty lot by breaking the sled loose. The runners are frozen fast."

Hal followed the man's advice. The overloaded sled moved ahead to where the path turned and sloped. As they swung on the turn, the sled tipped over, and it spilled half its load.

"Whoa! Whoa!" cried Hal. Onlookers caught the dogs and gathered up the things. They told Hal and Charles that they could take only half the load if they ever expected to reach Dawson.

Hal and Charles cut the bulk in half and bought six more dogs. This brought the team to fourteen. The new dogs did not amount to much, and with the team so worn out; the outlook was anything but bright.*

The men, however, were cheerful and proud. Never had they seen a sled with so many dogs! What Charles and Hal did not know was that one sled could not carry the food needed for fourteen dogs.

As the days went by, Buck realized that the two men and the woman knew nothing. And they were too lazy to learn. Some days it took half the morning to pack up and get moving. Other days the group was unable to get started at all. Charles and Hal argued over who did the greater share of work. Mercedes rode on the sled instead of walking because she was tired.

Then one day Hal realized that the dog food was half gone, and his team had covered only a quarter of the distance. He cut down the dogs' daily shares of food and tried to travel more miles each day. But it was impossible to make the dogs travel faster, and the late start in the mornings kept them from traveling longer hours.

After many days of travel and not enough food, the dogs began to die of starvation. Finally only five of the fourteen dogs remained.

Buck pulled when he could. When he could no longer pull, he fell down and remained down. Then blows from a whip or club drove him to his feet again. His fur hung limp where it wasn't matted with dried blood. Every bone in his frame showed through his hide. It was heartbreaking to see, but Buck's heart was unbreakable.

It was beautiful spring weather, but neither the dogs nor the people were aware of it. Dawn arrived by three in the morning. Twilight lasted till nine at night. The whole long day was a blaze of sunshine. Leaves were in bud. Squirrels chattered in the trees, and birds flew overhead. The earth was thawing, and from every slope came the trickle of running water.

Amid all this new life, under the blazing sun and through the soft breezes, staggered the two men, the woman, and their team of huskies. At last they came to John Thornton's camp at the mouth of White River. The dogs dropped down as though they had all been struck dead. Mercedes, who had been crying, dried her eyes. Charles sat stiffly on a log while Hal did the talking.

John Thornton was putting the finishing touches on an axe handle that he was whittling. He warned Hal not to take any more chances on the melting ice. "I wouldn't risk my life on that ice for all the gold in Alaska," he said.

But Hal only sneered and uncoiled his whip. "Get up there, Buck! Mush on!"

At first the dogs did not get up. The whip flashed again and again. Several times Thornton started to speak, but then he held back. Even when the other dogs managed to rise, Buck made no effort. He sensed danger out there on the ice where his master was trying to drive him. Buck had made up his mind—no matter what happened he was not going to get up.

Buck's refusal to move drove Hal into a rage. He swapped the whip for the club, but still Buck refused to move. As the blows continued to fall, the spark of life within Buck flickered and nearly went out. Suddenly John Thornton sprang upon Hal, pushing him backward. "If you strike this dog again, I'll kill you," Thornton said.

"That is my dog," Hal answered. "I'll kill him if I want. Now get out of my way. I'm going to Dawson."

Thornton, axe in hand, stood between Hal and Buck. Hal drew his long hunting knife as Mercedes screamed. Thornton used his axe handle to knock the knife to the ground. Then he stooped, picked up the knife, and cut Buck loose from the sled.

Hal had no fight left in him, and Buck was nearly dead. A few minutes later Hal and his team pulled away without Buck and headed down the river.

As Buck watched them go, Thornton knelt beside him and with rough, kind hands searched for broken bones. Buck and Thornton watched as the sled crawled over the ice. Suddenly the sled's back end dropped, and they heard Mercedes scream. Then a whole section of ice gave way. Dogs and people disappeared into the frigid water. A huge hole was all that was left.

John Thornton and Buck looked at each other, and Buck licked Thornton's hand.

Chapter 5

For the Love of a Man

When John Thornton's feet had frozen
that last December, his partners had made
him comfortable and left him to camp by
the river to get well. Then they had gone on
up the river to get a raft of logs. Thornton
was limping slightly when he rescued Buck.
As the weather grew warmer, Thornton's
slight limp disappeared.

Buck slowly regained his strength. He
lay by the river, watching the water and
listening to the songs of birds. Buck's
wounds healed, his muscles swelled out,
and the flesh came back to cover his bones.

*Skeet, a little Irish setter, and Nib, a huge husky, made friends with Buck and drew him into their games. They seemed to share the kindness of Thornton. Buck, Thornton, Skeet, and Nib all played as they waited for Thornton's partners to return.

Buck's love for John Thornton grew. Not only had Thornton saved Buck's life, but he was the ideal master. He looked after his dogs as if they were his own children. He had long talks with them. And he had a way of holding Buck's head in his hands, resting his own head next to Buck's, and shaking Buck playfully back and forth. Buck knew no greater joy than this rough embrace. Then Buck would take Thornton's hand in his mouth and gently press down with his teeth in a sort of hug.

Buck went wild with happiness when Thornton touched him or spoke to him. He* would lie for hours at Thornton's feet, looking up into his face.

For a long-time after his rescue, Buck did not like to let Thornton out of his sight. He followed closely at Thornton's heels. He was afraid that Thornton would slip out of his life like other men had done. Sometimes at night Buck would stand close, listening to the sound of his master's breathing.

But in spite of Buck's great love for Thornton, the instincts within Buck remained. He would not steal anything from Thornton, but he would steal from other men. And Buck fought more fiercely than ever, although he did not fight with Skeet and Nib, who belonged to Thornton.

Buck lay by Thornton's fire, a broad-breasted dog, with white fangs and long fur. But within Buck stirred the longings of his ancestors—half wolves and wild wolves. They called to him from his dreams. They called him deep into the forest.

When Buck heard the call from the forest, he turned his back on the fire. He plunged into the soft, unbroken earth and the green shade. Yet his love for Thornton always drew him back to man.

When Thornton's partners, Hans and Pete, finally returned, Buck accepted them. But he had love for Thornton alone. It was obvious that Buck would do anything for Thornton. "I'm not going to be the man that lays hands on you while he's around," Pete said one day as he nodded toward Buck.

Before the year was out, Buck proved Pete's statement to be true. Thornton was breaking up a quarrel when a man named Burton suddenly struck him. Buck leaped for Burton's throat. The crowd that drove Buck away saved Burton's life. But from that day, Buck's name was made. His name spread through every camp in Alaska.

In the fall, Buck saved Thornton's life again. It was on a dangerous stretch of rapids on the Forty Mile Creek. Thornton was in his boat, using a pole to move it along, and Hans and Pete were on the riverbank, guiding the boat with a rope. Buck, who was also on the bank, kept his eyes on his master.

At a rocky spot in the river, the boat flipped over. Thornton was flung from the boat and was carried downstream toward the worst of the rapids. It was a stretch of wild water in which no swimmer could live.

Buck instantly went to the rescue. Thornton grasped Buck's tail as Buck swam for the bank, but the force of the water pulled them downstream. Thornton clutched a rock and released his grip on Buck. "Go, Buck! Go!" he shouted.

Buck was swept downstream, but he finally reached shore. Quickly Pete and Hans tied a rope to Buck's shoulders and launched him back into the stream. When Buck got within reach, Thornton closed both arms around the dog's shaggy neck while Hans tied the rope to a tree.

Buck and Thornton were jerked under the water. Gasping for breath and smashing against rocks, they made their way to the riverbank. Buck had broken three ribs, but he had saved Thornton's life.

That winter at Dawson, another event put Buck's name many notches higher on the totem pole of Alaskan fame. Men were boasting of their favorite dogs. A man known as Matthewson stated that his dog could start a sled loaded with seven hundred pounds.

"Buck can start a thousand pounds," said Thornton. "He can break it loose from the ice and walk off with it for a hundred yards."

"I'll bet a thousand dollars he can't," said Matthewson slowly, slamming down a sack of gold dust that was the size of a sausage.

Nobody spoke. Thornton could feel his face getting red. He'd spoken too quickly. He did not know whether or not Buck could drag a thousand pounds. That was half a ton! And he did not have one thousand dollars.

"I've got a sled standing outside now with a thousand pounds of flour on it," said Matthewson.

Thornton glanced at Jim O'Brien, an old friend. Without thinking, he whispered, "Can you lend me a thousand?"

"Sure," answered O'Brien, slamming down a sack beside Matthewson's. "Though I'm not so sure your dog can do the trick."

Several hundred men gathered around Matthewson's sled. It had been standing for a couple of hours and had frozen fast to the hard, packed snow. No one believed Buck could do it.

"Three to one!" Matthewson shouted. "I'll raise the bet. What do you say?"

Thornton was doubtful, but his fighting spirit was aroused. With help from Hans and Pete, he was able to put up another two hundred. Matthewson laid out six hundred.

Buck was harnessed. He was in perfect shape, his coat shone like silk, and his muscles were hard as iron. The crowd fell silent.

Thornton knelt down next to his dog. He took Buck's head in his hands and rested his cheek on Buck's. "As you love me, Buck," he whispered. Buck answered him by taking Thornton's hand in his mouth and pressed gently on it with his teeth.

Thornton stepped back. "Now, Buck!" he said. With great effort, Buck jerked the runners of the sled loose from the ice. Then he hurled himself forward. His muscles knotted. His feet flew like mad, clawing against the hard, packed show. The sled swayed at first and then lurched ahead till it was moving steadily along.

Men gasped, and then they began to breathe again. Thornton ran behind the sled, cheering Buck. As Buck neared the end of the hundred yards, the crowd began to cheer and cheer. Hats and mittens were flying into the air. Buck had done it! Buck had moved the sled!

Thornton fell on his knees beside Buck. He rested his head on Buck's head, gently shaking him back and forth. Tears were streaming down Thornton's cheeks. "I'll give you a thousand for him, sir. A thousand, sir. Make it twelve hundred," he heard.

"No, sir!" was Thornton's reply.

Chapter 6

Back to the Wild

The sixteen hundred dollars in winnings made it possible for Thornton, Pete, and Hans to pay off their debts. After that, Thornton was able to journey eastward with his partners in search of a lost mine.

Many men had searched for the lost mine. Few had found it, however, and more than a few had never returned from the journey. The mine was said to hold the purest nuggets of gold, unlike any others in the Northland. It was said that an old cabin marked the site.

*Thornton, Pete, and Hans, along with Buck and half a dozen other dogs, sledded seventy miles up the Yukon to the Stewart River. Thornton was unafraid of the wild. He hunted for his dinner each day as he traveled. And if he failed to find food, he went on, knowing that sooner or later he would find some. Tools and ammunition made up most of the load on the sled, and it didn't matter to him how long the trip took.

Buck loved this hunting and fishing and wandering through strange places. Sometimes they went hungry, and sometimes they feasted. They camped here and there. The dogs loafed around, and the men washed pans of dirt to look for traces of gold.

Months came and went. Once the team found a path that blazed through the forest, and they believed the Lost Cabin was very near. But the path began* and ended nowhere.

Another time they came upon an old hunting lodge, and amid the shreds of rotted blankets, Thornton found a long-barreled gun from the old days in the Northwest. But there was no hint of the man who had left the gun.

When spring arrived once more, the group came to the end of their wandering. They did not find the Lost Cabin but a valley where the gold glistened like yellow butter across the bottom of the washing pan. Each day the men worked, they earned thousands of dollars in clean gold dust and nuggets. They sacked the gold, fifty pounds to the bag, and piled it up like firewood.

There was nothing for the dogs to do other than haul meat now and then, so Buck spent long hours by the fire. He often heard the call from the depths of the forest. It filled him with unrest and wild stirrings.

Sometimes Buck followed the call, barking and sniffing his way deep into the forest. Or he would hide behind the trunks of fallen trees, watching and listening.

Buck might be lying in camp, dozing lazily in the heat of the day, when suddenly his head lifted and his ears perked up. He dashed through the forests and along dry creek beds. He would lie in the underbrush for hours watching the birds. Above all he loved to run in the twilight, looking for something that called to him.

One night he sprang from sleep, his mane spiking. From the forest came a call— a long howl, familiar but unlike that of any husky. Buck dashed through the woods till he came to an open place among the trees. There he saw it—a long, lean timber wolf with its nose pointed to the sky.

Buck circled with friendly advances, but the wolf fled. After all, Buck was three times its size, and the wolf's head barely reached Buck's shoulder. Time and again the wolf was cornered, only to dash away again. But after some time, the two rubbed noses and played about. They ran side by side. Buck was wildly glad. He knew he was at last answering the call.

They stopped by a stream to drink when Buck remembered John Thornton. Buck turned and started back.

When Buck returned to camp, Thornton was eating dinner. Buck rushed upon him in a frenzy of love.

For two days and nights, Buck did not leave camp. He never let Thornton out of his sight. But then Buck's restlessness returned. He began wandering the woods.

Buck started sleeping out at night. He began staying away from camp for days at a time. He spent all this time searching for his wild brother. He killed his meat as he traveled. He fished in a stream. He even killed a large black bear. The blood-longing in him became stronger than ever before.

With his own strength and skills, Buck survived in a world where only the strong could survive. Because of this he carried himself with pride. It showed in every ripple of muscle and shimmer of fur. Had it not been for the stray spots of brown on his muzzle and the splash of white on his chest, he might well have been taken for a giant wolf.

"Never was there such a dog," said Thornton one day, as the partners watched Buck marching out of camp.

"When he was made, the mold was broken," said Pete.

They watched Buck leave, but they did not see what took place as soon as he was in the forest. Buck no longer marched. He became a thing of the wild, stealing softly among the shadows. He knew how to crawl on his belly like a snake. He knew how to leap and strike. He could take a bird from its nest. He could kill a rabbit as it slept. He could catch a chipmunk in midair. He killed to eat, and he liked to eat what he killed.

As the fall arrived, Buck came upon a band of twenty moose. The bull among them stood over six feet tall. Its antlers were seven feet across, branching to fourteen points. The bull was as challenging as any opponent Buck could desire.

Buck attacked and then retreated until he cut the bull from the rest of the herd. Then he stalked the great moose for days. Buck did not give the moose a moment's rest until he finally pulled it down. For a day and a night he remained by the kill.

Refreshed and strong, Buck headed back toward camp and John Thornton. But he sensed a change; he sensed danger. As he drew closer to camp, he moved carefully. The forest was silent. Birds had fled. The squirrels were in hiding.

Buck followed a new scent into a thicket. There he found Nib, lying dead, with an arrow sticking out of his body. A hundred yards farther, Buck found one of the sled dogs. From the camp came the faint sound of many voices, rising and falling in a singsong chant. Then Buck found Hans lying facedown, feathered with arrows like a porcupine.

At the same instant, Buck peered out where the lodge had been. He saw what made his hair leap straight up. Driven by his great love for John Thornton, Buck growled and rushed at the Yeehat Indians. In a frenzy to destroy, Buck sprang at the Yeehat chief. There was no stopping him. The arrows of the Indians were useless against him. The Yeehat Indians scattered far and wide over the country.

Buck now mourned his loss. He found Pete where he had been killed, lying in his blankets. Following the scent, Buck traced Thornton's struggle to the edge of a deep pool. There lay Skeet with his head and forefeet in the water. And hidden in the discolored water was Thornton's body. All day Buck mourned by the pool. He roamed about the camp. He knew Thornton was dead, and it left a great ache in him.

Night came, and a full moon rose high over the trees. From far away drifted a faint, sharp yelp, followed by a chorus of similar yelps. Buck rose to his feet. As the moments passed, the yelps grew louder. The call was stronger than ever before. And as never before, Buck was ready to obey. John Thornton was dead. His last human tie was broken. The claims of man no longer bound him.

The pack of wolves invaded Buck's valley. Into the moonlit clearing they streamed like a silvery flood. In the center of the clearing Buck stood waiting, as still as a statue. The wolves were awed at Buck's size and stillness.

Then one of the boldest leaped straight for him. Buck struck and then stood, unmoving, as the stricken wolf rolled in pain. Three more wolves leaped at Buck, one after the other. And one by one, they drew back, streaming with blood.

The whole pack moved forward, but Buck was everywhere at once. At the end of half an hour, the wolves drew back. Then one lean, gray wolf advanced in a friendly manner. Buck knew him as the wild brother with whom he had run for a night and a day. They touched noses.

An old, battle-scarred wolf stepped forward. Buck sniffed noses with him. The old wolf sat down, pointed his nose at the moon, and broke into a long howl. The others joined him. And Buck, too, sat down and howled.

The pack crowded around Buck, sniffing. Then the leaders darted away into the woods, yelping, as the others followed. And Buck ran with his wild brother, yelping as he ran.